W9-BKE-236

MIGHTY MIKE
REPAIRS A Playground

By Kelly Lynch   Illustrated by Casey Lynch

magic Wagon

visit us at www.abdopublishing.com

For Esther, who loves to play. –KL
For Daisy –CL

Published by Magic Wagon, a division of the ABDO Group, 8000 West 78th Street, Edina, Minnesota 55439. Copyright © 2011 by Abdo Consulting Group, Inc. International copyrights reserved in all countries. All rights reserved. No part of this book may be reproduced in any form without written permission from the publisher.

Looking Glass Library™ is a trademark and logo of Magic Wagon.

Printed in the United States of America, North Mankato, Minnesota.
092010
012011
♻ This book contains at least 10% recycled materials.

Written by Kelly Lynch
Illustrations by Casey Lynch
Edited by Stephanie Hedlund and Rochelle Baltzer
Cover and interior layout and design by Abbey Fitzgerald

Library of Congress Cataloging-in-Publication Data

Lynch, Kelly, 1976–
   Mighty Mike repairs a playground / by Kelly Lynch ; illustrated by Casey Lynch.
          p. cm. -- (Mighty Mike)
   ISBN 978-1-61641-132-9
[1. Repairing--Fiction. 2. Helpfulness--Fiction. 3. Community life--Fiction.]   I.
   ch, Casey, ill. II. Title.
        L9848Mr 2011
          2

                                                                 2010016265

It was a simmering summer afternoon, and Mighty Mike had just finished a hard week of work.

"I sure am tired!" he exclaimed. "I can't wait to get home and go to bed. I could sleep all weekend!"

Just then Mike heard a *bump*, a *thump*, and a *clunk*. The noises were followed by a little voice saying, "Ouch!"

Mighty Mike looked around. "Are you all right?" he called out in his booming voice.

"No!" squeaked a small voice. It came from the playground!

"Wait right there," Mike answered. "I'll help you!" Mighty Mike ran to the playground. When he got there, he found sweet little Daisy and helped her up from the ground.

"Daisy!" Mike exclaimed. "What happened?"

Daisy answered, "I was climbing the ladder to the top of the slide when one of the steps broke. I fell. But don't worry, it happens all the time. A lot of the equipment here breaks."

"All the time?" asked Mighty Mike with a frown. Mike looked at the playground. The slide was in shambles, the jungle gym was junk, the teeter-totter was trash, and the monkey bars were a mess. In fact, the entire playground was in disrepair!

"Everything in this playground is broken," Mike said. "What happened?"
Daisy explained that no one ever fixed the playground. "It's been like this as long as I can remember," she told Mighty Mike.

It didn't take Mike long to realize that he wasn't going to have a nice, restful weekend. If he didn't fix the playground, somebody was going to get hurt, and soon!

The next morning, Mighty Mike drove to the hardware store and loaded his big truck with lumber and nails. Then he drove back to the playground and unloaded everything.

Where am I going to start? Mike thought. *There are so many things to fix!*

The more Mike looked, the bigger the job got. But Mighty Mike knew that if he didn't get started, the playground would never get repaired. First, he replaced the steps that led to the top of the slide.

"There!" he said as he smacked the last nail into place. "Now Daisy can climb to the top without falling."

Next, Mighty Mike put a new plank on the teeter-totter and tightened the center pivot. When he was done, he tipped it back and forth to make sure it didn't squeak.

Just like new, Mike thought.

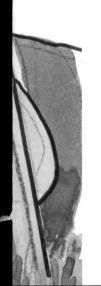

After repairing the teeter-totter, Mighty Mike fixed the swings. He hung new chain and replaced the seats.

"These were an accident waiting to happen," Mike mumbled as he worked. The shiny new chain and sturdy seats made the swings as good as new.

Glossary

accident - an unplanned event.

appreciation - an expression of admiration, approval, or gratitude.

disrepair - in need of being fixed.

pivot - a pin on which something turns.

plank - a heavy, thick board.

satisfaction - a state of being content.

shambles - a scene or state of destruction.

What Would Mighty Mike Do?

• How does Mighty Mike find out the playground needs repairs?

• Why does Mighty Mike decide to fix the playground?

• How does Mighty Mike repair the playground?

• How does Daisy know Mighty Mike did the repairs?

But Mighty Mike had worked so hard repairing the playground that he was fast asleep in his office. In fact, he was sleeping so hard that he missed the phone call and the lunch that they had in his honor. But don't feel too bad for Mighty Mike, lunch that day was toasted sardine sandwiches, and that's not exactly his favorite!

"Mighty Mike did this?" asked the mayor. "Well, we must do something for him to show our appreciation. Today he will be our special guest at lunch!" And the crowd cheered.

Early Monday morning, a crowd gathered at the playground. When they saw their new equipment, they just stared. Everyone was wondering who had fixed everything.

Right then Daisy came running up. "I know who repaired our playground!" she said as she tried to catch her breath. "It was Mighty Mike!" She told everyone about falling off the slide and how Mighty Mike had helped her.

Mike worked hard all weekend. By Sunday evening, he had repaired, replaced, and repainted everything in the playground.

"There," Mike said, smiling with satisfaction. "Now the playground will be safe for the kids. But am I ever tired!"